TWIN TROUBLE

by Luke David
illustrated by Barry Goldberg

Simon Spotlight/Nickelodeon

KLASKY CSUPO INC.

Based on the TV series *Rugrats*® created by Arlene Klasky, Gabor Csupo, and
Paul Germain as seen on Nickelodeon®

SIMON SPOTLIGHT
An imprint of Simon & Schuster Children's Publishing Division
1230 Avenue of the Americas
New York, New York 10020

Manufactured in the United States of America

First Edition   10 9 8 7 6 5 4 3 2 1

ISBN 0-689-82624-9

"Give me that rattle, Phillip!"
yelled Lil. She gritted her teeth.
"No, Lillian. It's MINE!" yelled Phil. He
curled his lip and snarled at his twin sister.

"Is not, Phillip!" said Lil. "The rattle is MINE!" Lil pulled with all her might. Phil pulled with all his might. The rattle went flying to the other side of the room.

"WAAAAAAAAGH!" wailed Lil.

"WAAAAAAAAGH!" wailed Phil.

"Holy smokes!" said Betty, picking up her twins. "I know my pups like to bark, but . . ."

Lil reached across her mom to pinch Phil. Phil reached over to pinch Lil back.

"WAAAAAAAAGH!" both twins screeched at once.

"That's it," said Betty. She dragged Phil away from Lil and gave him to Didi.

"For once that old windbag might have a point," said Betty. "We *have* been acting like the twins are attached at the hip. Maybe that's what's eating them. Come to think of it, Howard dressed Phil in Lil's clothes yesterday and vice versa. We didn't even notice until bathtime."

"Oh, dear," said Didi. "Y'know, Lucy Carmichael dropped a box of hand-me-downs off the other day. Maybe you can find some outfits in there that encourage each twin's individuality."

Betty changed the twins' clothes. "Bingo!" she said.

"Interesting choices, Betty," said Didi. "You're defying gender stereotypes by encouraging imaginative play in Phil and professional aspirations in Lil!"

"Yep," agreed Betty. "These new togs are just the ticket."

"And no more two-for-one toy sales for us!" said Betty. She handed Lil a dump truck and Phil a baby doll. "It's different toys for you two from here on in!"

"Oh, brother!" said Lil to Phil.

"And now for the final stage in my game plan: separation!" continued Betty. "Deed, you take Phil upstairs, and Stu will take Lil down to the basement!"

"Well, all right, Betty," answered Didi, "but I'm afraid the twins will miss each—"

Betty checked her watch. "Gotta go. Time for my power swim around the lake. See ya!"

"WAAAAAAAAGH!" cried Lil to Chuckie. "I miss Phillip."
"It's all right, Lil," said Chuckie. "Just pretend I'm Phil."
"Okay, Chuckie," said Lil. "You can eat that waterbug if you want. I don't mind."

"Lil, yuck, that's disgusting!" said Chuckie.
"Face it, Chuckie," said Lil. "You're not even a teensy bit like Phillip. I miss my twin brother!"

"WAAAAAAAAGH!" cried Phil to Tommy. "I miss Lillian."

"It's okay, Phil," said Tommy. "Just pretend I'm Lil. Whaddya say we eat these dust bunnies?" Tommy popped a dust bunny into his mouth. "Plegh!" He spit it out.

"No, Tommy," said Phil. "If you want to be like Lillian, you gotta swallow it." Phil popped a dust bunny into his mouth, chewed it, and gulped. "Num-num!"

"WAAAAAAAAGH!" cried Phil to Tommy. "I still miss Lillian."

"Don't worry, Phil," said Tommy. "I have a plan." Tommy picked up his cup-and-string phone. "Come in, Lil! Come in, Chuckie. Over and out!"

"This is ground control, Major Tommy," answered Chuckie.

"We gots to get these twins back together," said Tommy. "Make a break for it and rendez-moo in the kitchen in oh-five-jillion-seconds."

"Copy," answered Chuckie. "Over and out."

"Lil, Chuckie," said Stu, "do me a favor and wait here while I run Dil's new and improved Kangaroo up to the kitchen."

"Eureka!" said Lil.

"Drat! My dad's new high-security stair-gate is up!" said Tommy.
"But don't worry, Phil. I have a plan!"

"Funny, this basket seems heavier than usual," said Didi as she lugged the laundry downstairs.

All the babies met in the living room.
"Lillian!" yelled Phil.
"Phillip!" yelled Lil.

"Nothin' seems any fun without you," said Phil.
"Being a twin is a prettyful thing," said Lil.

"We tried to keep them separated," explained Didi, "but they do seem happier together."

"Well, you know what I've always said," said Betty. "When twins are happy, everyone is happy."